OH BEANS!
St★rring Half-Baked Bean

BY ELLEN WEISS • ILLUSTRATED BY SUSAN T. HALL

Troll Associates

Maybe you know somebody who's always rushing into things—never thinking about what *might* happen, never looking before he leaps.

If you do, then you know someone just like Half-Baked Bean.

Now, that's not to say that Half-Baked Bean isn't a wonderful fellow—he is. Everybody loves him.

Even though he never reads directions.

Even though he's always forgetting something.

Even though he's always getting stuck in corners.

One day, not very long ago, Half-Baked Bean had an idea. "Hey, everybeany," he said, "let's go camping! Wouldn't it be wonderful, sleeping under the stars—"

"—In our nice cozy sleeping bags," said Vanilla Bean.

"Sleeping bags?" said Half-Baked Bean. "I forgot about them."

"And we'll need some tents, won't we?" said Boston Bean.

"Oh, right, tents," said Half-Baked Bean. "I forgot about them."

At last they were off. They went up a hill, down a hill, around a lake, through a valley, and into the woods. Half-Baked Bean was always first, charging ahead to see what was around the bend.

"Let's go deeper into the woods," Half-Baked Bean said excitedly.

"My feet hurt!" snapped Snap Bean. "Let's stop here and rest."

And that's just what everyone did.

"It's really pretty around here," said Vanilla Bean. "Wherever we are."

"Where are we, anyway?" Boston Bean asked.

"I know where we are—WE'RE LOST!" snapped Snap Bean.

"Why don't we look at the map?" Boston Bean suggested.

"Map?" said Half-Baked Bean, looking around. "I forgot about that."

"Well, this is an awfully beautiful spot," Vanilla Bean said sweetly. "Let's set up our tents, build a fire, and cook a wonderful dinner!"

"Oh, right," said Half-Baked Bean, "I—"

"DINNER?" yelled everyone. "You forgot about DINNER?"

"This is really the very last straw!" Boston Bean yelled. "Now we have nothing to eat for dinner!"

Half-Baked Bean felt awful.

"Let's look on the bright side," Vanilla Bean said. "The woods are full of good things to eat. There are nuts and berries—"

"And Half-Baked Bean is going to find them—OR ELSE!" snapped Snap Bean.

While Half-Baked Bean went off to find dinner, Boston Bean sat down on a large rock. A very, very large rock.

"R-R-R," said the rock.

"R-R-R-ROARRRR!!!"

"A grizzly bean!" they all screamed. "A great, big, frightening grizzly bean!"

"With bad breath!" coughed Vanilla Bean.

"What should we do?" yelled Bean Sprout.

"Run! Hide! Panic!" screamed Boston Bean.

Meanwhile, Half-Baked Bean was poking around the forest, looking for things to eat.

"Aha!" he said, spying a great big honeycomb. "Honey for dinner! Just the thing." And he picked it up and headed back to his friends.

When Half-Baked Bean returned to the campsite, he was in for quite a shock. "Yikes! A fearsome grizzly bean!" he exclaimed.

"Do something!" yelled Boston Bean.

Half-Baked Bean didn't waste too much time thinking about a plan. As usual, he just sprang into action.

"Here, catch," he said, throwing the honeycomb to the grizzly bean.

The grizzly bean looked pleased when the honeycomb landed in his paws. It was dripping with sweet, golden honey.

But just as he reached inside, a bunch of angry bees buzzed out.

Suddenly, he was surrounded by them. He let out a yelp and ran off into the woods.

"Hooray!" yelled everyone. "You rushed right in and saved the day!"

"Shucks," said Half-Baked Bean. "I was just lucky. But I learned my lesson. From now on, I'll think things through. No more dumb mistakes for me."

Half-Baked Bean kicked the ground, a little embarrassed. Then he said, "Hey, look at these pretty leaves."

He picked them up and held them out to his friends.

"Oh, no," screamed the other beans.
"POISON IVY!!!"
Half-Baked Bean had done it again.